BILLIONAIRE'S CURVY BET

BY

ANNABELLE WINTERS

Copyright Notice

Books by Annabelle Winters

The CURVES FOR SHEIKHS Series
Curves for the Sheikh
Flames for the Sheikh
Hostage for the Sheikh
Single for the Sheikh
Stockings for the Sheikh
Untouched for the Sheikh
Surrogate for the Sheikh
Stars for the Sheikh
Shelter for the Sheikh
Shared for the Sheikh
Assassin for the Sheikh
Privilege for the Sheikh
Ransomed for the Sheikh
Uncorked for the Sheikh
Haunted for the Sheikh
Grateful for the Sheikh
Mistletoe for the Sheikh
Fake for the Sheikh

The CURVES FOR SHIFTERS Series
Curves for the Dragon
Born for the Bear
Witch for the Wolf
Tamed for the Lion
Taken for the Tiger

The CURVY FOR HIM Series
The Teacher and the Trainer
The Librarian and the Cop
The Lawyer and the Cowboy
The Princess and the Pirate

WWW.ANNABELLEWINTERS.

BILLIONAIRE'S CURVY BET

BY

ANNABELLE WINTERS

1

<u>INDIA</u>

He will ask you a question . . .
  And your answer must be No.

The moment I see his ring I know this is a setup. Not sure *who* is being setup, but it's still a fucking setup. I should call the cops and the FBI right now and end this. End *him*, if that's what it takes to get my money back.

Not just my money but my power, my self-respect, my hard-won victories, I think as I feel the man's gaze on my curves while I try to ignore him and focus on my drink. He *is* handsome, I'll give him that. Not my type, though. He's got player written all over that arrogant smile, those dark green eyes, that long, lean body he's angling in my direction.

"My name's India," I say when it's obvious he's about to talk to me anyway. No point in pretending. I just wanted to make sure this was the guy Mother and Father expect me to meet. The guy who's going to ask me a question. A question to which the answer is No. Should be easy enough.

"I need to ask you something," the man says after introducing himself as Ingram.

"No," I say quickly. "The answer is no."

Ingram flinches like I just slapped him across the face, and when I see a flash of panic in those cool green eyes, I know he's in the same boat as I am. His assets and property seized or locked down, bank accounts erased, credit cards blocked, safety deposit boxes sealed. All because we joined some secret society back in college. Can't believe I was so excited to be one of the first three women to be accepted to the Society. How could I have been so stupid?! That weird induction ceremony where we were all summoned to a hotel room and lectured by recorded messages from a man and woman who called themselves Mother and Father? How could I not have realized I was joining some psycho cult run by lunatics! Hell, I'm surprised Mother and

Father haven't asked me to sacrifice a cute little piglet under the full moon. Though maybe that's coming next.

"I haven't asked you the question yet," Ingram says, rubbing his smooth jawline and narrowing his eyes at me.

"What difference does it make?" I say. "I have to answer no or else I'll be in line at the soup kitchen by the end of the week. In this fucking dress."

Ingram snorts, and then he glances at my dress and shrugs. "They'll probably let you cut in line. I sure as hell would." He flashes a smile, but then blinks and goes serious. "In fact I might be in line with you by the end of the week. Especially if you say no to what I'm supposed to ask."

I stare for a moment, and then I swallow hard and nod. My gaze softens, and I speak quietly. "Mother and Father?" I say.

Ingram nods. "Who the fuck are they?"

I look down at my ring. Then I look at his ring and frown. "Why are you asking me?" I say. "You should know. You're clearly been part of the Society longer than I have."

Ingram raises an eyebrow. "You calling me old, little girl?" he growls.

I almost smile. He's most certainly older than

I am, but he clearly doesn't care. And that flirty, growly voice as he looks into my eyes . . . huh . . . maybe he *would* be my type under different circumstances. Maybe when this is all over . . .

"Let's just get this over with," I say. "What's the question you're supposed to ask?"

But Ingram shakes his head like he's not sure if he's ready to ask it. I think a moment, and then I snap my fingers.

"All right. How about you just *tell* me the question instead of asking," I say, beaming because I'm so damned smart. Always was the smartest, starting from grade school. Except for that whole I-joined-a-crazy-cult-by-mistake thing, of course.

Ingram raises an eyebrow and touches his chin. "So if I *tell* you the question, it won't count as *asking* you the question."

"Correct," I say. "That way we can talk about it."

Ingram looks at his platinum Rolex. Then he looks out the tinted window of the Club and squints. "I guess I have some time." He takes a slow breath and looks me square in the face, his green eyes shining almost like he's excited, like he's relishing the challenge of whatever it is Mother and Father want him to do. "They made a bet . . ." he says, leaning close enough that I pick up his masculine scent, a natural aroma of cedarwood and tobacco leaf that catches me off guard.

And then my guard is broken down and trampled by what comes next.

"They bet I couldn't get you to marry me by sunset," Ingram says. "That I couldn't get you to say yes. Couldn't get you to be mine."

I stare like he's speaking in tongues, and then I shake my head and smile like I'm hoping this is all a dream. "Well, you . . . you *can't*," I say, blinking in confusion. "Who gets married to someone they just met?"

Ingram shrugs. "They do that in arranged marriages, don't they? Those usually work out."

"I don't know if *usually* is the right word," I say, wondering what the hell kind of cult has got their claws into me. "Anyway, I am not having this discussion. Not with you, at least. I should have my head examined for not calling the FBI already."

"Relax," says Ingram, tapping his ring on the bar to get the bartender's attention. A moment later a glass of dark single-malt scotch slides across the polished bar. He tosses it down like a kid drinking cranberry juice, and then he turns to me and smiles. "I've already got the FBI, the NSA, and everyone in between working on it." He glances at his gold-plated phone that's sitting silently by his glass. "I expect a call any minute informing me that all my accounts are back."

I shake my head and smile up at him. He's cool on the outside, but I can see the turmoil behind those green eyes. Somehow that makes me relax a little. I'm not sure why. Maybe it's the sense that I'm not alone in this.

The word "alone" echoes in my head as we share a moment of silence, like we're both hoping our phones ring and it turns out to be a prank or a glitch or maybe a tear in the fabric of the universe that's now been sewed up and smoothed out. But nothing happens, and I get the distinct sense that's what's *supposed* to happen: Nothing.

Nothing until we face each other and play this game.

I glance at his phone and then back up into his eyes. "Would it help if you called your FBI contacts back and told them the same thing just happened to me?"

"Maybe," says Ingram without making any move towards that phone.

"Um, so how about we do that?" I say.

Ingram rubs his jaw and raises an eyebrow. Then he exhales and shakes his head. "No," he says, his voice oozing authority, like he just made a decision that's final, binding, set in stone, inked in blood.

"OK . . ." I say slowly, trying to sound calm. "And . . . and why?"

He smiles slowly, those green eyes narrowing. "Because they bet me I couldn't get you to marry me by sunset. And I have a hard time backing down from a bet."

I widen my eyes and wait for him to say something that actually makes sense. But he's just smiling like a wolf, staring like I'm his prey, breathing like he's on the hunt. Then he reaches out and touches my hand, sending a spark of electricity through my body, a wave of excitement that makes my thighs tingle, my toes curl, my nipples stiffen. It's the gentlest of touches—just his fingertip on my knuckle. But it feels like I've been struck by lightning, tapped by fate, dinged by destiny.

Again the word "alone" rings in my head like a solitary wedding bell. I've been alone for what feels like forever, and although it worked well for me while I climbed the ladder, smashed through the glass ceiling, claimed the wealth and power that I deserved, lately it hasn't been working so well for me. Turns out there's no shortage of gold-digger men out there, and for the first time in my life I realized that money can sometimes get in the way of love.

Well, money can't get in the way here because there is no money, I think as I stare into Ingram's eyes to check if he's serious or just seriously insane. But then I break the eye contact and shake my head when I remind myself that I'm the crazy one if I get distracted from the real goal here: Get my damned millions back!

"You have a hard time backing down from a bet?" I say, repeating Ingram's words just to make sure I'm hearing correctly. "This isn't a game, Ingram."

Ingram exhales and leans in just a little. "Maybe it is a game," he says, furrowing his brow and nodding. "Mother and Father seem to know that I'm a betting man, that I see a bet as a challenge, a chance to prove myself right and prove the other guy wrong." He pauses, looking at me in a way that makes me uncomfortable but in a weirdly good way. "And I bet they know something about you too."

"Really? Like what?" I say.

"You tell me," he says. "Your task was simply to say no, correct?"

"Yes," I say. Then I smile. "I mean no. You know what I mean."

He grins, his handsome face lighting up and lighting me up with it. For a moment I almost forget that this isn't a date but is instead some twisted criminal prank that I can't believe we're even engaging with.

"Let's just play along for a minute," Ingram says. "What happens if you say yes and we do get married by sunset?"

I swallow hard and think. "Well, considering I was instructed to say no, I assume there will be consequences for me."

"Consequences to marrying me? Damned right there'll be consequences. All of them good," he whispers, totally flirting with me even though this isn't the fucking time.

I shake my head and try to hold back my smile. But it breaks through anyway, and suddenly we're both grinning like idiots—which means we probably *are* idiots, given the enormity of what's happening.

"OK, I'll take this seriously," Ingram says, still smiling. "Consequences for you . . . let's see. I assume that means Mother and Father won't give you your money and assets back if you don't turn me down. You agree?"

I nod. "I assume that's their game."

"And what kind of assets are we talking about?"

Ingram says. "Ball park figure. A million? Ten million?"

I close one eye and scrunch my face up. "More," I finally say. "A lot more."

Ingram's eyes go wide and he stares for a minute. "Seriously?" he says, glancing down at my smooth bare arms, my brown shoulders, that hint of cleavage.

"Is that surprising?" I demand, clenching my fist below the bar and reminding myself that breaking his sexist nose probably isn't helpful right now. "You arrogant piece of—"

"Whoa! Timeout!" Ingram says, waving the conversation dead and turning bright red. He rubs his jaw and exhales hard. "I guess I deserved that. I guess a part of me made the totally unacceptable and sexist assumption that any woman who looks so fucking hot in a red dress can't also have tens of millions of dollars in the bank."

I'm still fuming, but the sad truth is that I've seen the same subtle prejudice even from other women, some of whom have even quietly asked if I had an older husband who died without getting me to sign a pre-nup. In a weird way, Ingram did a little better because he seems to accept without question that I earned my millions the American way: By working my ass off for ten long years, sacrificing every other part of my life along the way.

"Is that supposed to be a compliment?" I ask with raised eyebrows. "Because it's not. You pretty much just said that a hot woman can't also be smart, powerful, and wealthy."

"That is absolutely *not* what I said," Ingram says firmly. "I meet smart, powerful, wealthy women who are hot as hell all the time. Problem is, they're all either crazy or married. So which one are you?"

I shake my head in disbelief. "You don't know when to stop, do you? Nope. You just keep doubling down on your own arrogance and ignorance," I say.

Ingram shrugs. "I always double down. Told you I was a betting man. And speaking of bets, can we get back to the topic at hand before you punch me in the face and we both get arrested for fighting?"

"Wouldn't be much of a fight," I say, holding up my fists and sporting a mean look that makes my nose tickle. "I've knocked out bigger, badder wolves than you."

Ingram grins, holding his hands up in surrender. "I don't know if that's a joke, but since you're wearing red like Little Red Riding Hood, this wolf isn't taking any chances."

"I thought you were a betting man," I say, holding the tough-girl look and throwing a slow, fake punch at the big bad grinning wolf.

Ingram grabs my wrist, and when I playfully swing with my other hand he swiftly takes hold of my other wrist. Now he's got me trapped, and a wave of heat passes through me when I feel how strong he is—and how he's controlling that power in a way that makes me feel safe with him, like he's my best bet out of this crazy situation.

Problem is, I think as we smile at each other and he lets me go, that might put me in an even crazier situation.

"Sorry to burst your billionaire bubble, but you aren't marriage material," I say, straightening out my hair and sipping my non-alcoholic drink which is way too sweet. I was kinda-sorta teasing but not really, sorta-maybe flirting but of course this isn't the time and he isn't the guy.

Though *could* he have been the guy if we'd met under different circumstances, I wonder as Ingram dismisses my jab with a grunt and taps on his empty glass with that black Society ring.

"How many drinks is that?" I say, frowning as Ingram knocks back another scotch like it's a jello-shot at a frat party.

He stares at me like I'm an alien, and his face

clouds over like he can't believe I just said that. Shit, I can't believe it either. What the hell do I care? Ohmygod, would I be *that* kind of wife if we got married?!

Now I'm all messed up in my head because suddenly I'm thinking about marrying Ingram. Not thinking about it like I want it. I don't think so, at least. I don't want it. Do I? I can't want it. Can I?

"So I'd have to stop drinking when we get married?" Ingram says, a lopsided smile breaking on his face as he touches my arm with the back of his hand.

The contact gives me goosebumps, and I look away to hide my smile. Thankfully my brown skin makes it easy to hide my blush; still, I can't hide from the annoying fact that I'm actually attracted to Ingram. Not to mention the vaguely flattering fact that he's attracted to me. I saw the way he checked out my ass when I walked in here, and I remember how my nipples stiffened when I looked into those eyes and saw what was going on in his filthy mind. Shit, maybe in a different life this could have been something. An evening of fun, if nothing else.

"Still nothing," says Ingram, looking at his phone and then his watch. "That's not a good sign if even my contacts at the FBI haven't got a lead." One more glance at the sun through the window and then he faces me. "And we haven't got much time, India. Look, even not doing anything is a decision. If we just sit here like fools until the sun goes down, we both lose."

I shake my head and smile. "Nope. You lose. I win. I had to say no to your question, and if we aren't married by sunset, it means I've said no."

Ingram grins and slowly shakes his head like he's got me in his wolf-trap. "I haven't asked you the question yet," he whispers through that wicked grin. "And until I ask, you can't answer. So we're in a deadlock, a stalemate, a game of chicken with our entire net worths on the line. That get your blood pumping, little girl?"

My blood does pump a bit harder, most of it going to my head and throbbing in my temples. He's technically right, I realize. He *told* me the question, but he didn't actually *ask* it yet. And I can't answer a question that hasn't been asked. Asshole is right. If we do nothing, we might both lose.

My mind spins through the possibilities, most of which seem to be lose-win situations: One of us needs to lose for the other to win. Which of course is a problem when you've got two ambitious, competitive people who are used to winning and sure as hell don't like to lose.

I wonder if there's a win-win scenario, and I try to ignore the little whisper at the back of my mind that maybe marrying Ingram is the winning play. I almost hate myself for having that thought, and I have to excuse myself and head for the restroom to get my head straight.

The Ladies Room has a lobby with a plush purple couch in the center of it, and I collapse into the soft suede and stare up at the ceiling. It's painted black and dotted with scores of pin-sized lights that make it feel like a starry night in here. Soon I'm lost in my thoughts, and I find myself thinking of something Ingram said about arranged marriages and how common they used to be for like . . . well, forever, actually. Marriages based on love are a pretty recent invention . . . and one that's somehow resulted in a divorce-rate that would make an alien wonder why humans insist on doing something that doesn't seem to work out very often.

That little factoid is part of the reason I've avoided marriage like the plague, I think as I stare up at the starry ceiling. And with my net worth, a divorce would be fucking expensive.

"Ohmygod," I mutter, frowning and pulling at my lip until it hurts. "Have I denied myself the chance of falling in love because I'm so darned logical and analytical? Did I overthink it to the point where I believe the stats that most marriages fail and therefore decided that it makes better financial sense to just never get married? Have I been unconsciously making the safe bet with my own life, my own wealth, my own . . . heart?"

I sit up straight on the couch, gasping as I feel something click inside me (in a good way . . . I think). It really feels like this train of thought is going somewhere—and that it's somehow connected to what's happening.

"Is that what Mother and Father are doing?" I whisper out loud. "Trying to force us to confront ourselves, face up to the beliefs that have been holding us back from happiness?"

As if in response, my phone beeps and a message pops up. It's my accountant, and my heart skips like three beats when I see the text:

Good news! One of your smaller accounts just popped back online! Hopefully the others will be back soon! The bank's cybercrime team is working with the FBI, and hopefully it's just a glitch that'll be fixed by end of day. By sunset, the lead FBI person says.

I'm relieved at the message, but at the same time a weird tension tugs at me from the inside. I read the message again, frowning when I see the word "sunset" at the end. Weird. What kind of FBI agent would give an estimated timeframe for solving a case and set the deadline at sunset?

And then I get it.

I get the message.

Not the message from my accountant, but the message that's hidden in there. The secret message from Mother and Father. That the clock is ticking. The deadline is looming. What are you going to do, India? Say yes to an arranged marriage and no to your wealth?

I think about the way Ingram smelled, the way he touched me, the way he looked at me. I imagine our children, with his eyes and my skin. I imagine . . . ohmygod, stop!

"Stop!" I shriek in horror when I realize that I'm actually scared of saying *no*! I'm actually considering letting him win his bet and seeing what happens! No way. Just . . . no. Stop. Reset. Breathe. "I've dedicated my entire life to earning those millions! I paid the price! How can I somehow be thinking about marriage and togetherness and a future with a man when my entire past just got stolen from me?! I can't do this. I need to talk to someone about this before I do something I can't undo, before I know *why* I feel this way."

2

INGRAM

"**Y**eah, why not," I slur to the bartender as he points at my empty scotch glass. But when he tops it off I stare at the whiskey and then push the glass away.

A sloppy grin breaks on my face, and I almost laugh when I realize that India got to me with that frowny comment about my drinking. It's fucking ridiculous that I let a woman exert her will on me like that, but a part of me loves it even though another part is pissed off.

"Where is she, anyway," I grunt, looking at my watch again and then glancing over towards the hallway. I grin as I remember how I stared at her ass like a pervert who hasn't seen a woman in years.

Fuck, but India makes me feel like I haven't seen a woman in years—not a woman like that, at least. So damned pretty, with that angelic round face and those dynamite brown eyes that ooze intelligence and wisdom. This woman is a keeper, and I want to keep her.

Keep her forever.

"That settles it—you're drunk like a monk," I mutter, the memory of India's hips swaying through in my head. My cock hardens as I indulge in the fantasy of pulling that red dress off her, seeing what lies beneath that thin satin. Fuck, how I'd love to take my time exploring her body, touching her in ways I bet she's never been touched, making her feel things no man would even dare imagine.

Soon I'm lost in the fantasy, my head in the clouds, a goofy grin on my face, India's aroma filling my senses. I can almost feel her smooth skin on my palms, her silky hair between my fingers, her warm cunt sheathing my cock as I place her on my lap and bounce her up and down while I suck those boobs, bite those nipples that I bet are big like saucers. And then I'd lose myself in those eyes when I come, kiss those lips as she comes, pull her close and tell her she's mine, all mine, fucking *mine*!

I almost slide my ass off the barstool, and when

I come to my senses I realize I've drooled down my chin. I glance down at myself, hoping to hell I didn't just explode in my pants like a frustrated teen having a wet dream in his bunk-bed. Nope. Although my cock is stretching the seams of my tailored trousers, clearly it's holding out hope that I'm gonna make good on that fantasy.

"It's not that simple, buddy," I whisper to my cock before quickly glancing around to make sure nobody's close enough to see that Ingram's lost his mind. Lost his mind over a woman in a red dress.

Now I'm on my feet, and I start to pace around the mostly empty lobby. I feel warm and feverish, uncharacteristically uncool, my emotions swinging between mad arousal for India and wild anger at the situation.

But as I pace like a tiger in a cage, it occurs to me that I'm barely thinking about the money situation, about potentially losing my billions, about being broke, wiped out, my life's work stolen. For some reason that seems like the least of my worries right now. The situation that's driving me nuts isn't about wealth. It's about a woman.

I stop pacing so abruptly I almost fall over, and I stare down at the silk paisley carpet and rub the back of my head. I'm shocked that I'd actually forgotten about the money for the few minutes when I imagined being with India, tasting her lips, smelling her hair, feeling her skin against mine. Hell, now I'm doing it again!

And then suddenly I *roar* with laughter, pump my fists in joy, hop up and down like a lunatic at the beach. "Mother*fucker*!" I shout, grinning wildly as the most liberating thought blasts me off to outer space in a love-rocket drawn by unicorns.

Then I bound towards the women's room as the bartender shakes his head and tries to pretend he didn't see that. Somehow I manage to stop myself from barging in headlong and probably getting pepper-sprayed and then arrested. But I need to see India, tell her that I just saw the light, figured it out, realized that Mother and Father wanted to show us how easily we could forget about wealth when presented with a future full of love for a person instead of love for money.

Suddenly I'm certain India came to the same realization, that she's imagining being with me, being loved by me, claimed by me. She's probably shocked at how easily she could forget about a lifetime's worth of wealth when presented with a lifetime's worth of love.

"Of course, we won't need to choose between

wealth and each other," I say to myself as I straighten my tie and glance down at my crotch to make sure it doesn't look too obscene. "Mother and Father just wanted to force us into a situation where we had to face parts of ourselves we've been denying for decades. Just like God teaches lessons by creating events in the world of men and women and seeing how His kids navigate the situation."

I bang on the door and wait, but there's no answer. I frown and cock my head, but just as I'm about to walk in and tell India that she's mine and once we're married Mother and Father will turn the lights back on with our wealth, a waiter calls out to me from the kitchen door at the end of the hall.

"That's the women's room, Mister Ingram," he says nervously.

"I know," I growl. "My wife . . . I mean fiancée . . . I mean girlfriend . . . I mean . . . hell, I don't know what I mean. I just need to talk to the woman in red, OK?"

I wave the freckle-faced waiter back to the kitchens, but he stands there gulping like a goldfish.

"She . . . she left, Mister Ingram," he stammers. "Walked out through the kitchen. Right out the loading dock."

I blink and raise an eyebrow, and then I'm running like my life depends on it. I don't know why I'm running, but it's too late to stop.

Luckily the waiter leaps out of the way, and I slam through the swinging doors, plow through the sous-chef, and blast through the open loading dock like a superhero about to save the day.

The sunlight startles me, and when I see how low the sun is, I realize that sunset is looming like a ticking timebomb. Suddenly all that clarity I had about Mother and Father and learning lessons and getting our money back disappears, and I stumble through the street looking around like a shell-shocked soldier.

"India!" I shout, my mind whipping itself up into a frenzy as I try to figure out where the fuck she went and *why* the fuck she went! Does she not see that Mother and Father put us together for a reason? Does she not see that the situation was designed just for us? Why did she run? How does that make any sense?!

I start to panic, wondering if something happened, if Mother and Father aren't our Fairy Godmother and Godfather but instead exactly what they appear to be: Crazy cult leaders who like to toy with their victims before crushing them with the death-blow. Either that or they're demons— and they've taken my angel from me.

Finally I get a hold of myself and stop my frantic search so I can think. I didn't become a billionaire by freaking out and losing my shit at every setback or obstacle. If Mother and Father just wanted to steal our money, they would have done it without saying a word. Clearly this is a game, and clearly I haven't won yet.

I glance over at the sun again, and I feel my competitiveness spark up, sense my confidence swell, my belief in my own power come back. I smile when I realize that all the adrenaline got me sober like a sundial. And my smile breaks to a wide grin when I also realize that I still don't give a fuck about the money. If I had to start from scratch, I could claw my way back to the Big B again. Mother and Father can stuff that money up their gloryholes for all I care. I'm going after the one thing that can't be replicated, can't be duplicated, has no substitute in this world.

I'm going after love.

As for marriage?

I'm going after that too. Except the deadline is meaningless now. I already know what I want out of life, *who* I want out of life. I want India, and if I have to wait a day to make her mine, so be it.

Yup. Since I've emotionally let go of my attachment to the money, Mother and Father can't pull the puppet-strings, have no hold on me. I just won the game by changing the rules.

By making it *my* game.

And just as the thought completes itself, my phone beeps. It's my accountant with an update:

Great news! A smaller account popped back online. FBI is working on the rest, and the lead guy says it should be fixed by sunset if everything goes as planned.

"Fixed by sunset if things go as planned," I mutter as I read the message. "Is it weird that the FBI said it'll be fixed by *sunset*? Why the fuck would they say that? Is this a hidden message from Mother and Father? Are they reminding me that the game is still on, that if I lose the bet I'm going to lose not just the money but something else—something more valuable?"

Suddenly it occurs to me that the very first message from Mother and Father said I'd *already* lost some unknown bet. If so, what if my money is already gone forever, if the wealth was the price I paid for losing the *first* bet?

I start to pace through the streets as a chill slithers up my back like a snake. Because if Mother and Father already took my billions for some unknown first bet that I lost, what of value do I have left to put on the line for this second bet?

"I got it wrong," I mutter, clenching my jaw as that chill spreads to my back and around to my chest, making my heart pump cold blood through my veins. "I've already lost my money. It's not coming back, no matter what I do. Which means that I'm wagering something else that's precious to me. But what? Without my money I have nothing of value. Nothing but my wallet, my clothes, my watch . . . and my life."

Only now do I think back to what I remember about the Society, about that strange induction ceremony with a recorded message narrated by someone called Father. It was decades ago, and I sure as hell can't remember the details. But one thing that stuck with me was how Father said joining the Society wasn't a life membership—it was a *forever* membership. There was also something about sunset or sundown or twilight in that message, wasn't there? It had seemed like over-the-top flowery stuff you see in Fraternity rituals, so Hayes and James and I had shared a good laugh after it was done.

"I should call Hayes," I mutter, dialing his number and then sighing when it goes straight to voicemail. I shoot him a quick text to call me back, and then I call James, the only other member of the Society, far as I know at least.

James is usually upbeat and high-energy, but he sounds tense as fuck right now. Something's clearly wrong, and I sense that Mother and Father and the Society are fucking with him too. Hell, I bet that's why Hayes's phone is off: He's probably mixed up in some carnival ride of a game too!

For some reason I relax a little. Knowing all three of us Society guys are being played gives me some solace, and I decide to let James know I'm in the same shit. At first he pretends he doesn't know what I'm talking about, but I push harder and he confesses.

And what he confesses almost makes my heart stop.

"They gave me a contract," James says. "And I have to deliver on it by sunrise, or else I lose my billions forever."

I snort and smile. "A contract? Lemme guess: Marriage contract with a woman from the Society."

"No," says James. He goes silent, but I can hear

him breathe. "A contract on you, Ingram. On your life."

3
<u>INDIA</u>

"**N**ot on your life," I say to Janelle. "Marry some-one after one meeting? And did I mention he drinks Scotch like water?"

"There's your problem," says Janelle, dropping two cubes of ice into each glass of spring water. "You're a perfectionist. You know what they say about the obsessive search for perfection, right?"

"No. What do they say about it?" I ask, smiling as I take a sip. I called Janelle from the taxi I hailed when I snuck out through the loading dock past the Club kitchen. She was one of the three women who joined the Society a decade ago—and the only one I'm still in touch with. No idea what happened to Hannah. She might be dead, for all I know. Hell, she might be Mother, for all I know!

"Fuck if I know," Janelle says with a shrug as she slides herself onto the teardrop shaped leather couch. "But I'm sure it's something."

I laugh, releasing some of the nervous energy of the day. But certainly not all of it, and I feel the tension tighten my shoulders as I wait for Janelle to react to all the shit I just threw at her about the Society, Mother and Father, missing money, and some kind of game in which we don't know the rules and don't know what's at stake.

Janelle looks at her phone and then sighs and puts it away. "Well, I haven't gotten any messages from Mother and Father. And my millions are still where they're supposed to be," she says, taking off her glasses and smiling like she's trying to stall long enough to decide whether I'm crazy. "Should I withdraw everything and hide the cash under my bed just in case I'm next in line?"

"I know you're kidding—and I know you think *I'm* kidding—but this is fucking real, Janelle," I say. "What the hell kind of cult did we join like airheaded idiots? We were smart enough to build business empires on our own, but somehow dumb enough to get involved in something like the Society?"

Janelle sighs and puts her glasses back on. "Well, given the situation, obviously it was a dumb thing to do. But back then it seemed exciting and kinda neat—being the first women accepted to an ancient secret society and all. And there was nothing about lifetime membership dues or anything like that."

"Maybe because it wasn't a lifetime membership but a *forever* membership—whatever the hell that means," I say. "And why do you say it's an *ancient* society? Do you know about its history? I couldn't find anything online about it."

Janelle shrugs. "Maybe not ancient, I guess. But I do remember during the induction ceremony recording there was something about the Society's origins being in the world's oldest university. What is that, Harvard? So like the 1600's? Old, but not ancient."

I shake my head. "Harvard might be America's oldest university, but it's not the oldest in the world. The first university ever is debatable, but I remember reading a theory that it's actually in India. An ancient city of learning that was used by Buddhists and all kinds of other religions or groups. Started in 500 BC or something."

"BC?!" says Janelle, her eyes going wide. "Huh. That is kinda ancient. India, you said? That's an ancient country that's now the data-center and cloud-computing capital of the world." Her back straightens and she stares at me. "It's also your name. Are you Indian?"

I glance down at my brown arms and do a half-shrug, half-nod. "Maybe. Probably. Don't know for sure. Never got one of those ancestry tests." Janelle's about to ask the obvious question about my parents, and I stop her with the not-so-obvious answer. "I was adopted. In America. No records of my birth parents—I've looked."

Janelle frowns. Then she cocks her head and looks at me askance, like she's wondering if I'm playing a trick. "You know I was adopted too, right?"

I blink and stare as a chill rises up my spine like a viper. I bite my lip so hard it almost bleeds. Both of us being adopted could be a coincidence. But what about the third woman? Hannah? Three for three would be too much to be a coincidence.

So I grab my phone and scroll through my contacts, sighing when I come up empty. "Hey, do you have Hannah's number? You remember Hannah, right?"

Janelle's distracted by her own phone, and I figure she's about to call Hannah to see if being adopted is a common thread. But when I see her frantically tapping on the screen and then standing up abruptly and yelling into the phone, I know it isn't Hannah.

It's Mother and Father.

Pretty good timing, right?

Almost like they could hear us.

Can they hear us?

I look around the room, wondering if this place is bugged. Of course, nowadays the listening bugs are the size of a pinhead, and you can't find them without a scanning device. But then I stare at my silent phone blinking on the table, and suddenly it occurs to me that you no longer need to hide bugs in rooms anymore—not when everyone is carrying a high-definition recording and transmission device 24-7. It's called a phone, and every tech company tracks our every move, word, and maybe even every thought. If the Society can make our millions go away, surely they can tap into the networks that feed into our phones.

I consider turning off my phone and tossing the battery away. But then I remember how one of my accounts popped back online, and I decide it might be better if they're listening. Besides, I think as I glance out the window, I get the creepy feeling

Mother and Father are watching and listening in some other way, a way I don't even wanna think about.

"What twisted little game do they have you playing?" I finally say, leaning back and sipping my water as Janelle tosses her phone at the couch and furiously runs her hands through her dark hair.

"It's not a game," Janelle says as she paces the room, her face ashen, her fingers curled into tense fists. "They said I've been given a contract, and I have to deliver on it by sunrise tomorrow or else my millions will disappear into the clouds."

I shrug and nod. "My game was to answer a question. Ingram's game was to win a bet. Your game is to deliver on a contract. Lemme guess: Marriage contract with some asshole billionaire from the Society?"

I smile to lighten the mood, but Janelle's expression is dark as sin. Slowly she shakes her head, and the lightness evaporates as that chill in my spine rises up to my throat and grips tight.

"No, not a marriage contract," she whispers, walking to the window and turning her back to me. "A death contract." When she turns, I almost don't recognize Janelle. Her red lips are tight like wires, her brown eyes narrowed to slits, her eyebrows twitching like there's something under her skin. "A death contract on you, India. Mother and Father want me to kill you before the sun rises in the East."

4
__INGRAM__

"Kill him before the sun rises in the East," I say, reading from the message on James's phone. I look over at him and toss the phone back. "That's pretty fucking clear. No reading between the lines there."

"Correct," says James, stroking his jaw and eyeing me up and down like he's sizing me up, wondering if my body will fit into his Louis Vuitton luggage or if he'll have to dice me up and run me through a blender before pouring me down the sink.

I look around the sprawling downtown penthouse that occupies the top three floors of this highrise. Pretty sure James owns the building too.

Motherfucker hit the Big B in spectacular style when he bought depressed real estate during the last recession and rode the recovery right to the top of the mountain. He's legit, just like Hayes and me.

But that's where the comparison ends, I think as we lock eyes and ride the tense silence in the spartan postmodern room with panoramic views of the early evening sun. Yup, although all three of us can be tough as nails in a negotiation, arrogant as fuck in an argument, confident to the point of narcissism in our personal lives, James always had a edge to him—an edge darker than anything that lives in Hayes or myself.

But he's not a killer, I think as we both break grins at the same time and share a fist-bump across the old metal chest that doubles as a coffee table. The thought of actually killing me hasn't even crossed his mind—which is why we're here at his place, strategizing about how to track down Mother and Father and end this game. Interestingly, Mother and Father haven't locked down James's accounts yet, which makes me wonder if we're missing something about his game.

Don't forget that your own game is counting down, I remind myself as I squint into the glare of the evening sun. But I can't think about that right now. I've already decided that India is mine, and if I lose all my money, so be it. I'll just climb back up the mountain again. Besides, I don't even know where that woman in the red dress is hiding. And anyway, given that the game has advanced to putting out death contracts on people, it's best India stays hidden while I figure this shit out.

"What I can't figure out is why they haven't locked out your accounts yet," I say as James offers me a drink—which I decline. I need my wits about me right now. Besides, who knows what's in that drink . . .

James shoots back the drink he just offered me, smacking his lips as if to prove it's not poison. "Because if they'd taken my billions we wouldn't be having this conversation," he says matter-of-factly. "Hard to talk when your dead body is being chilled in my meat freezer."

I see the twinkle in his green eyes and laugh out loud. There's an edge to the humor, but it's probably a good thing we're joking about it. It's almost exciting, actually—probably because it keeps the adrenaline going. "Nice," I say. "Right next to the ribeye."

We share another laugh, and then James goes

serious. "Why do *you* think Mother and Father haven't locked my accounts like they did with you and . . . what's her name?"

"India," I say, frowning as a fiercely protective instinct rises up. Immediately I'm back to obsessing about why she left the Club, where she might be, what might be in store for her. "Fuck, I need to find her, James."

"You think she might be in trouble?" James says.

"Well, we're *all* in trouble," I say with a grunt. "But we need to stick together, figure this out as a team."

"I'm not much of a team guy," James says. "Neither are you, far as I remember."

"This isn't the time to reminisce about our glory days," I growl. "I can't get a hold of Hayes, and you're the only other Society member I know. It's just the three of us guys. And India, of course. Maybe that woman who's with Hayes right now. Anyone else you know of?"

James nods. "There is another woman," he says slowly, stroking his chin. "I met her briefly at a conference last week, actually. She had a Society ring on her finger, which struck me as strange, since the Society didn't accept women, far as I knew. So I assumed it was her husband or boyfriend's ring, and obviously I cut the conversation short even though she was smoking hot, sexy as hell, with hips like heaven. But I don't do married women." He snorts and raises his shot glass. "Or marriage, for that matter. But that's a different conversation."

"Maybe not," I say. "Maybe it's the same conversation."

"What do you mean?" says James.

I think for a bit. "Well, both of us have spent considerable energy avoiding marriage," I finally say. "Why is that, you think?"

"Coz marriages are doomed to fail. What the fuck kind of question is that?" James shakes his head, looking at me like I've lost it.

I shake my head too, but clearly Mother and Father want all of us to think about marriage, that ancient institution that's the foundation of society, the smallest unit of a family. Two coming together as one, merging their separate pasts to create a united future.

"Did your parents have a bad marriage? Did they divorce when you were a kid?" I ask.

James rolls his eyes. "Fuck, I should kill you just for asking lame-ass questions like that. What are you, my therapist?"

"Just answer the question," I growl. "I think Mother and Father want us to face our beliefs about marriage." I rub my jaw and glance off to the left as I think back to when James and I were younger and would take those trips to Vegas—which, ironically, is Ground Zero for insta-marriages. "You remember that night in Vegas when we saw a drunk couple heading to a wedding chapel?"

"Vaguely," James says with a grin. "What about it?"

"Well, I remember you asked me if I'd ever consider getting hitched," I say, shaking my head and smiling. "I said I'd rather die. You remember what you said next?"

James stares wide-eyed as the memory comes back. "I said I'd rather . . . kill."

Now I'm wide-eyed too, but with excitement. "So you said you'd rather kill than get married. And I said I'd rather die than get married. Now we're in a game where if I don't get married by sunset, I might die by sunrise . . . killed by you."

"Sonofabitch," James mutters, biting his lip and staring out the window as the sun moves ever so slowly toward the horizon. "So the guy who says he'd rather die than get married is killed by the guy who says he'd rather kill than get married. Mother-*fucker*! That's so brilliantly twisted I almost like it!"

"Easy for you to say," I say with a grin. "I'm the

guy with his ass on the line." We share a laugh, and now I'm on a roll. "But now that we've figured out the game, we know how to win it. You get it, right?"

James frowns as he taps the space between his eyebrows. "We have to do what we swore we wouldn't. Or else Mother and Father will hold our billions hostage until we do what we said we'd rather do."

"Exactly," I say, slapping the tabletop and making the shotglass jump. "So if I marry India, I win the bet and get to live. And if you get marred to the woman Mother and Father choose, then you're released from the death contract, which means you no longer have to kill me to keep your billions."

James nods, and then he shakes his head. "So my choice is either marry some woman I don't even know or else put a fucking bullet in your head to get out of it or do nothing and go broke? That's a sick-ass choice, bro."

I shrug. "You *did* say you'd rather kill than get hitched," I remind him.

James stares at me poker-faced. "What if I decide to stick by that statement?" he says softly, in a way that's only ninety-percent fucking with me. Then he blinks and smiles. "Just messing with you, of course. But those choices are pretty heavy, Ingram.

Marriage? I guess I could get married and divorced, but who knows if that would satisfy Mother and Father. Yeah, I don't know, man. At least you've met your match."

"And I bet you've met yours," I say. "That woman with the curvy hips and the Society ring. You actually remember her from a few weeks ago, which is unusual for you. Women don't stick around in your roving mind—or in your life, for that matter."

"Janelle, her name was," James says, and I see a spark behind those dark green eyes. She made an impression, I can tell. Just like India sparked something in me. Just like that curvy woman caught Hayes's attention in the most electric way. That's three for three. Pre-ordained matches that feel like fate, meant-to-be, straight-up magic.

As if by magic, both our phones beep at once. We're both lightning quick on the draw, and a moment later we're holding our phones up and comparing messages.

"Same message," I say. "A set of GPS coordinates. Same coordinates." I think a moment and then cock my head and look up. "Is it possible India and Janelle are together right now?"

James types in the coordinates and shrugs. "That new condo building. Not far from here." He glances at the sun and then winks at me. "Sun's still up. Let's see if we can save your billionaire ass in time."

5
__INDIA__

"**T**here's no time for that," Ingram says urgent-ly, grabbing my wrist and whipping me around to face him. "The sun's on its way down. We need to do this now, India. I told you, I don't think our money's at stake any longer. It might be our lives. If we aren't married by sunset, it's going to set off a chain-reaction of conditions in this fucked-up game of matchmaking."

I'd been shocked when Ingram and James knocked on Janelle's door, and even more shocked when Ingram excitedly explained how Mother and Father were using his and James's own words as the conditions of the game.

But I wasn't as shocked about the game as I was about the words.

Words that I'd used myself a long time ago.

"Janelle, do you remember that bachelorette party down in Atlantic City just a couple of years after grad school?" I say. She nods, and I can see those words are as fresh in her mind as they are now in mine.

"You said you'd rather die than get married," Janelle says. She pauses, and her voice drops an octave. "And I said I'd rather kill someone than get married to someone." She shoots a quick look at James. "Nothing personal," she says, almost flirting with him in a way that makes this crazy situation feel vaguely surreal, almost playful, even magical.

"Um, *I'm* the one who should take it personally," I remind her, smiling as I think back to the scare Janelle gave me with that look. Janelle's always had a dark edge to her, but not *that* kind of dark. No way.

"Are we finished here?" Ingram says, one hand still on my wrist as he checks something on his phone. "Fuck. City Hall closed at five. Maybe we can call a Justice of the Peace at home. Or maybe fly to a different time zone fast enough."

I glance over at Ingram, and then I look down at

the way he's holding my wrist. His grip is surprisingly tender, but at the same time firm and unyielding. He'd seemed wired at first, but now I realize it's excitement, not panic. It's almost like he actually *wants* to do this.

Suddenly I'm taken back to that moment at the Club, when I faced my own prejudices and beliefs about marriage. And while I haven't suddenly changed all my beliefs, I can't help but feel that *something's* changed.

Is it because I'm no longer analyzing marriage as an abstract idea based on statistics and anecdotes and instead looking at it with a specific man in mind? Am I drawn to Ingram because of the heightened urgency and feverish excitement of the day? How can I analyze all the data fast enough to make a decision that's gonna impact the rest of my life?!

My breathing starts to quicken, and I shift restlessly on my feet as all those old habits of sitting alone in a room and overthinking my life to death make me sick to my stomach with anxiety. Overthinking and overanalyzing has always been a problem bordering on obsession, but it's what got me to the top of the corporate world. How can those same skills not work in this situation?!

"How is this gonna work?" comes Janelle's voice

through my head-chaos. She glares at Ingram and steps towards us like she's protecting me—or maybe her money. "The two of you said you'd rather die than get married. The two of us said we'd rather kill than get married. So you think if you two get married, you're not gonna die. And if James and I get married, we're off the hook for killing you. So that's it? We do that and everyone gets their money back?"

Ingram shakes his head and smiles. "No," he says softly. "My billions are gone forever. And once India marries me, her millions are gone forever too. I think that's the point of the Society's games. I think that's what Mother and Father are trying to show us, that's the lesson they want us to learn. That money isn't happiness, wealth isn't a goal, riches don't make you rich." He looks down into my eyes, and I feel the warmth of his gaze cut through the chill in the room. "And there's only one path to that lesson. You can't learn it from a book. You can't learn it by overthinking and overanalyzing. You have to *feel* its truth. You have to *live* its truth. And you have to live it forever. With all your commitment. All your heart. All your love."

I'm melting like a glacier in the sun, and I feel myself open up to Ingram. What he just said about overthinking and overanalyzing feels like it was meant for me. It's quieted down my furiously chugging brain, and soon all I can see are Ingram's eyes, all I can feel is his touch.

"Heartwarming speech," James says, making both Ingram and I glare at him like we wish *he* was dead. "But although you two might be on the way to deciding that having each other is enough, I sure as hell am not waving my billions goodbye and riding off into a happily-ever-after as a broke-ass nobody."

"Neither am I," says Janelle, glaring at James for a moment like she's offended. "And although the intention would be sweet and romantic in a movie, this is reality, hon. A reality where Mother and Father are criminals with connections and power. James and I still have our money, and we don't know for sure what will happen at sunrise."

"When the sun rises in the East," I say, absentmindedly repeating Mother and Father's words. Again the phrasing strikes me as odd, and although I try to dismiss the feeling, it sticks with me.

"Yeah," James is saying, glancing at Janelle briefly but long enough to check out her strong curves with approval. "We're just guessing that getting married will end this game in our favor. But although you're a betting man, Ingram, I like a sure thing. I can't just shrug, get married to someone I don't know, and then wait for Mother and Father's decision. In fact I should move all my money right now, pull out as much cash as I can just in case."

"My thoughts exactly," Janelle says, tapping her phone. "I'm calling my private banker to give them a heads up."

Soon both James and Janelle are talking to their bankers and arranging massive withdrawals. I shake my head when I remember that Mother and Father are probably listening. Interesting that they haven't wiped out their accounts like they did with me and Ingram. Even more interesting if Mother and Father let them withdraw millions in cash or bearer-bonds or whatever.

"I guess I'd do the same in their situation," I say, not sure if I believe what I'm saying. I'm super-aware of Ingram standing next to me, and I can't help feeling closer and closer to him even though we just met. Every moment I spend in his presence is making that vision of a future with him more clear, clearer than the present reality, brighter, more vivid, like my future self is whispering to me through the mists of space and time.

"Just in time," Janelle says, hanging up the phone and smiling in relief. "My banker was about to go home for the day, but she's gonna take care of things for me."

"International Bearer Bonds in million-dollar de-nominations," James is saying to his banker. "Clean out all liquid assets. Sell the stocks and bonds on the Asian markets which just opened. Don't worry about the property and hard assets for now, I guess." He hangs up and nods. "All right, even if Mother and Father wake up angry and vengeful tomorrow, I'll still have almost a hundred million in bearer-bonds that can be cashed anywhere in the world." He looks up at Janelle, his face taut, an edge to his grim smile. "Now we have till sunrise to find Mother and Father and make sure they don't wake up at all." He holds up his phone and grins before whispering into it. "You hear that, Mommy and Daddy? Your kids are coming for you, and you need to be afraid. Very fucking afraid." He nods at Ingram and shoots me a quick glance. "I think we should stick together tonight. We might need each other. We can't trust the police or FBI until we know more about who Mother and Father are—or at least where they are. Maybe we can trace some of the headers from their texts and get a location."

Ingram shakes his head. "I already had some of my guys do that. They say everything traces back to some cloud server in India—which is where pretty much *all* the world's data is stored nowadays. That location is meaningless. Mother and Father could be anywhere on the fucking planet. Where do we even start to look?"

I sigh as I feel Ingram let go of my wrist. That warm, almost magical moment is gone, and I touch my hair and sigh again as Janelle and James's behavior brings me back down to earth. Now I'm analyzing again, and the conclusion is that they're doing the logical thing. Maybe we're *all* doing the logical thing by going after Mother and Father instead of looking within ourselves for the answer.

I almost slip back into the safety of my analytical mind, but just before I give in to "common sense," Ingram slides his arm around my waist and gently pulls me close. He's looking at me like he wants to go, to leave these two to their own game, their own journey. We have our own journey to complete, and a thrilling sense of adventure lights me up from the inside when I realize how darned excited I am to be stepping out into the unknown realm of not being rich, not being wealthy, not being . . . alone.

Never being alone again.

I love this feeling, I say with my eyes as my body tingles from being so close to Ingram. I never want to lose this feeling. Not now that I have a glimpse into what togetherness might feel like. I might be wrong, but it's worth taking the chance on something that feels this wonderful even when the material world is crumbling like a house of breadsticks.

My smile fades a little when I see the big, orange-red sun sinking lower in the sky, and I feel a tug inside as I sense the clock ticking. But it's not anxiety or panic that's pulling at me. It's an understanding of myself that's creating the need to seal this deal by the deadline. There's a feeling that if Ingram and I don't do this under the pressure of the deadline, we might never do it. If Mother and Father gave us a week or a month or a year to "get to know each other" or some shit, we might fall back to the familiar old thoughts and habits that kept us locked up in our private worlds of wealth, power, and loneliness. Somehow Mother and Father knew they had to put us in a high-pressure situation with so many winding loops and hairpin turns that our intelligence gets exhausted and we simply surrender to our feelings, surrender to our emotions, surrender to each other. They understood that sometimes too much choice, too much freedom, too much analysis about an ideal mate can be counterproductive. As a society we've put the intelligence of the brain on a pedestal and ignored the wisdom of the heart, and maybe Mother and Father want to remind us that the heart rules matters of love and marriage, just like it secretly has for thousands of years, even when all marriages were arranged.

After all, many arranged marriages weren't *forced* marriages. Most families arranged a meeting and let the boy and girl see each other, look into one another's eyes, sense the rhythms of their breathing, the synchronicity of their hearts. In a way a lot of arranged marriages were love-at-first-sight marriages, weren't they? Is that what Mother and Father are getting at with these deadlines and red herrings and teases of danger and darkness? Just trying to get us out of our own heads, break us out of our routines, make us see that wealth and power and freedom comes not from an overflowing bank account but an overflowing heart?

Just then Ingram squeezes me gently around the waist, and I know instinctively his mind just met my mind in that silent world of thoughts and feelings. Our hearts just met in that secret world that hides beneath the humdrum of everyday life. And those hearts are so full they're overflowing. I feel it like a flood in my soul, a wave in my energy, a splash in my spirit.

Ingram and I slowly move toward the door. We haven't said a word, and Janelle and James are on the computer looking something up. There's no reason to be stealthy about it, but I'm getting a kick out of sneaking out. More than just a kick, though. There's also an undercurrent of danger that started when I saw Janelle's sinister expression earlier today and got stronger when I saw that James has the same dark edge to his energy. It doesn't seem like they're going to marry each other before sunrise. They aren't even close to looking inside themselves and facing whatever beliefs Mother and Father want them to face. They're focused on solving the problem in the external world, and that could be dangerous. Is it possible that these two together might consider doing something that either of them alone would never do?

"Let's do it," comes Janelle's voice in a sharp whisper, and I whip around in panic, all jumpy from that last thought. I notice that both she and James are checking their phones, and I seem to remember hearing twin beeps of messages coming in just a second ago. Did Mother and Father just text James and Janelle? What did they say? Why aren't James and Janelle telling us?

Janelle finishes talking to James under her breath, and when she turns to us she's smiling.

"Hey, India, remember when we were talking about the Society maybe having its roots in . . . India?"

I frown as I think back. "Yeah, but now I'm not sure why I thought of that—maybe it's the spiritual undertones of all this that made me think of India."

"Maybe it's your name," says Ingram. "Are you Indian?"

I shrug. "Don't know. I was adopted, remember? Oops. Sorry. Forgot we don't know each other that well yet."

Ingram frowns. "You were adopted? Huh. Me too."

I blink and glance over at Janelle. Then I turn to James. "Um, by any chance . . . were you also . . ."

James looks up and nods. "Yeah. I was adopted too. What about it?"

"I . . . we . . . we don't know yet," I stammer. "But right now it looks like all of us were adopted. You think it's weird that we're all adopted kids being messed with by some mysterious couple called Mother and Father?"

"Weirder than anything else in this whole thing?" says Ingram with a grin. "Sure. Now can we go before the sun sets and we get struck down by lightning bolts from the clouds."

"You guys aren't going anywhere," James says, striding to the door and standing in front of it like a guardian from one of those old temples.

"Actually they are," says Janelle, standing next to James and completing the picture. "But they're going with us." She turns to James. "Your jet or mine?"

"Where . . . where are we going?" I say uneasily as Ingram holds me closer to his body.

"India," says James like it's obvious even though it's totally not.

"Why?" says Ingram with a frown. "Did you get a lead on something?"

"Something like that, yeah," says James, glancing over at Janelle and then back at us. "Shall we?"

I place my hand on Ingram's forearm as I think. There've been a few links to India in all this—one link being my name, I guess. Again I glance at the setting sun, and now it occurs to me that flying to India would be a nonstarter.

"That's a fifteen-hour flight," I say. "We'd all miss our deadlines. Unless you're planning to murder us during the in-flight movie."

James grins and shakes his head. "International Date Line," he says triumphantly. "We fly west over the Pacific Ocean. Then we cross the International Date Line, skip a day, and reset the clock on our deadlines."

"That doesn't work for us, bro," says Ingram with a snort. "We'd need a supersonic jet to get to the International Date Line before the sun sets on America—assuming that's the loophole you're thinking about."

"He wasn't thinking about sunset," I whisper. "That's our deadline, not his. Their deadline is sunrise, and the whole International Date Line thing might work for them."

We all go quiet, and suddenly I know both Ingram and I are imagining being killed in International Airspace, our bodies dropped into the Pacific Ocean. It's ridiculous, of course. But I can't shake the feeling that although James and Janelle on their own aren't killers, there's something about these two together that worries me.

Again my mind is revving into high gear as I squeeze Ingram's arm to stop him from doing anything rash. I tell myself we're just being paranoid, that no way is anyone getting killed in this game. But at the same time, I'm starting to believe that the chance of something bad happening isn't zero. It's unlikely, but possible.

I look up at Ingram and wonder if this is the

first and last day we'll have together, and when he locks in on me I see the same thought behind those burning green eyes. And now I wonder what I'd want to do if tonight is all we had. Can we live so completely in the moment that it doesn't matter what happens tomorrow? Can we let go of not just our attachment to money but also our attachment to life itself? Can we truly surrender to the belief that love is eternal, beyond life and death? That love is truly forever?

"It's not a lifetime membership but a *forever* membership," I whisper. Then I turn to Ingram and look at him like there's no one else in the room. "What would you do if tonight is all we had? If our forever ended at sunrise?"

Ingram frowns as a shadow passes across his face. "What are you talking about, India? These guys aren't gonna—"

"That's not what I mean," I say as the sun hits the horizon and starts to dip. "This isn't about James and Janelle. This is about us, our game, our life, our forever. And our choices. Look, Ingram."

I turn to face the picture window, and the two of us are bathed in the golden glow of the setting sun. I feel Ingram's tension as the deadline looms, but I've let go. I'm at peace. I know this is what Mother and Father wanted to teach us: How to let go of ourselves, leave the past behind, step into the future on our terms, just the two of us.

"Ask me your question now, Ingram," I whisper as the sun dips halfway beneath the horizon. "I'll win you your bet. I'll do it for you."

Ingram's breath catches as he turns to me and smiles. Then he shakes his head, smiles wider, and pulls me into his body. We watch the sun sink below the horizon, and in that moment I know we both made the winning choice. We're so satisfied in the present moment, this perfect point between day and night, past and future, always and forever, that we've shed all attachments to the material world, including the attachment to life. We're pure spirit in this moment. Pure energy. Pure love.

And as the sky glows red like an apple in the Garden of Eden, Ingram leans close and with his eyes asks the question. I answer with my smile, and in silent synchronicity we exchange our Society rings with the clouds as our witnesses.

Then, as twilight casts its shadow across our forever, he kisses me.

By God, he kisses me.

6
INGRAM

I see myself kissing her like I'm floating on those gold-lined clouds, and it's a moment that almost makes me believe in the reality of the spirit, that maybe there is something beneath the surface of life, something we can't see but can sometimes feel with the right person.

"This feels so right, India," I whisper as I break from the kiss and then go right back into her. This time I'm completely in my body, and the sensations rolling through me are so strong I have to fight to stay on my damned feet. "I feel so free, like I can suddenly see that our love exists in the eternal, that we've always been in love, will always be in love, that life and death can't change that. This moment feels so complete that I've lived more fully in one sunset than I have in every other event of my lonely life."

"Me too, Ingram," she whispers back. "I think that's where Mother and Father were leading us. They were trying to get us to strip away all attachments and face each other as naked souls."

I grin as my body serves up a tasty image of my wife's naked soul, with curves that would make angels blush and turn demons green with envy. I kiss her again as I tell myself that she's my wife now, that we're married—and we did it on our own terms. India's right: We didn't have to prove anything to Mother and Father; we had to prove something to ourselves. And we did, didn't we?

"You think they've forgotten where they are?" comes James's voice from the background of my blissful dream. But even the rude interruption can't piss me off now, and I squeeze my curvy bride's side, kiss her deep and hard, and then slide my arm around her waist as we turn to face Janelle and James.

"Oh, you guys are still here," I say with an over-the-top groan.

"And you guys are . . . married?" Janelle says,

closing one eye and tilting her head as she looks at India. "Is that gonna work for the game?"

"But they did it after sunset," says James, rubbing his jaw and grimacing. "I think that means they both lose. So what does that mean for us?"

Neither India nor I say a word. It's too hard to explain. James and Janelle are just starting their game, and they have no idea what kind of journey Mother and Father have planned for their fated butts. All I know is it's gonna have a touch of darkness to it.

A part of me considers just busting our way out of here and leaving James and Janelle to find their own way to forever. But another part of me senses that our story isn't quite wrapped up. Maybe I'm getting suckered into the weird coincidences and eerie synchronicities and those feelings of transcendental love, but if the next stop on this magical trip is India, I kinda feel like there's something there for a woman named India . . .

"I call window seat," says India like she just made the same decision.

I sigh and then nod at James. "All right," I say. "But I'll mix my own drinks, and you two are sitting where I can see you."

Janelle and James both laugh, but the laughs

have a nervous energy to them. I know James well enough to feel reasonably certain he wouldn't murder someone for any amount of money—and certainly not just to stay single, if that's the condition. I believe that about Janelle too—after all, she and India appear to have stayed friends for years. But these two together give off a different vibe, and although I can't put my finger on it, I suspect that's the reason Mother and Father put them together. There's something about their combined darkness that they need to resolve, and maybe that resolution lies somewhere in the ancient spiritual land of India.

Though India is now the data-center and cloud-computing capital of the world, I remind myself with a chuckle as we head for the door. "You guys know that India is a massive country with two billion people," I say to James as we wait for the elevator. "Why the hell do you think we'll find any answers there? All we have is a few text headers that traced back to a computer server in India. Is that all we have to go on?"

"They both got new simultaneous messages from Mother and Father earlier," India says, narrowing her eyes and flashing a knowing smile at Janelle. "You did, didn't you?"

James and Janelle glance at each other, and then

Janelle sighs. James takes a breath and clears his throat. "You guys remember when I yelled into the phone earlier?"

I grin. "Mommy and Daddy be very afraid!" I say in a squeaky voice.

"Exactly," says James, biting his lip in embarrassment at the memory of how he lost his cool. "And clearly Mommy and Daddy are *not* very afraid." He taps his phone and holds it up for us:

We're waiting at home for you. Don't you dare come empty-handed, though. Bring the entire family. Dead or alive. Love, Mother and Father.

India and I stare at the message and the attached GPS coordinates that pinpoint a location in India. Then we stare at James and Janelle. They both look mortified, totally ashamed that they hid the message from us. I'm not sure if their reaction is reason to relax or be even more vigilant. On one hand, it's a relief to see that they aren't stone killers. But the fact that they look so ashamed means that they may have actually considered the possibility of bringing us to the family reunion in body-bags.

"Chill," says James with a smile. "They said dead or alive, and alive is way easier for all of us."

I counter with my own grin. "Yeah, but if we show up alive, does it mean you guys lost the game?"

"You had to have considered that possibility,

Janelle," India says from right next to me as we get to the elevators. "Remember, your game is only just beginning. Mother and Father seem to be designing each game specifically for the players, to get them to face their own beliefs, to help them break free of those beliefs."

"Not all of us are head-in-the-clouds spiritualists like you seem to have suddenly become," Janelle snaps. She taps her foot and clicks the elevator call button like an impatient child.

"And you seem to have suddenly become a complete materialist," India snaps back. "You aren't even considering the possibility of opening your heart to the man Mother and Father believe is your match."

I join my wife in the shouting contest, glaring at James as I let him have it. "And you're no better, James. To hell with playing this game. We already know how it ends. Instead of hoarding bags of money and chasing clues across the world, just take a minute and look at each other. The answer's right here, buddy."

James shoots me a sneer. "The fanaticism of the recent convert," he says, sighing and shaking his head like he pities me. "It's great that you think you're in love and that your little ring-exchange in front of the sun is the greatest moment of your life, but tomorrow you're gonna wake up broke with a woman you barely know and you're gonna feel like the world's biggest idiot. She's no different from every other woman in your past, you dumb fuck. You're just another stupid—"

But he can't finish the sentence because I finish it for him with my right fist. I swing lightning quick, my anger rising so fast I can't stop myself. I get him square on the jaw, and although he's a big guy, I'm built like a tank and he staggers back.

Just then the elevator arrives with a ding, and when the doors open I kick James in the chest, sending him flying into the back of the elevator. Almost immediately India shoves Janelle past the elevator doors, and Janelle screams as she slams into the woozy James, taking him down to the floor with her momentum.

The two of them are all tangled up, and James is so out of it from the punch and the kick, he drags Janelle back as he tries to pull himself up. And as we watch, the doors silently close, and the elevator whisks them away to their game, their challenge, their forever.

India and I stare at each other, both of us breathing hard at the excitement. This certainly wasn't planned, but the way the elevator doors opened and closed strikes me as a very convenient coincidence.

Are elevators hooked up to the cloud now? Can someone control them remotely? I almost laugh it off, but just then both our phones beep in unison:

We're both smiling as we check our messages, but the smiles are wiped off our faces with one word:

Run.

We stare at each other, but just then the elevator dings again. There's no time to analyze the situation, and after I punched James's lights out and India sent Janelle flying, any chance of a rational, civilized discussion is out the window. I don't know if Mother and Father just pulled us back into the game or if I did it myself by losing my temper and using my fists. But there's no time to think.

It's time to run.

7
INDIA

We run like thieves through the hallway, excitement racing through me as Ingram grips my hand tight and busts through the fire-door into the metal stairwell. We barrel down the stairs like freaks, and by the time we step out into the underground parking lot, we're both panting and perspiring, grinning like dogs at the park.

Ingram looks around for the exit, and I point at the red neon sign at the far end. But before we take a step, a bubble-shaped red electric car pulls up in front of us and honks twice.

I squint as I try to get a look at the driver, and I almost faint in shock when I see that there *is* no driver! "Um, Ingram. Ingram. That car doesn't have a . . ."

"Sonabitch," Ingram says with a grin. "Self-driving car! A lot of tech companies have been running tests, but this is the first time I've seen one." He looks at the car and then turns to me. "You think this is . . ."

"Look at the license plate," I whisper, pointing with a trembling finger like a ghost identifying a murderer.

Ingram looks and then turns back to me. "JSTMRD?"

He gets it just as I say it out loud.

Just Married.

8
<u>INDIA</u>

Our little red wedding chariot cruises through the city like we're riding a cloud. Ingram's holding me against his body, and we're staring out the window like dreamy kids at Disneyland.

The self-driving car takes us downtown and uptown, past office buildings that we frequented in our old lives, through streets we walked down alone, so lost in our drive for wealth that we barely noticed the people. Had we walked past each other without noticing? Had we passed up the chance to find our forever many times before? Is that why Mother and Father took it into their own hands to cross our paths, cross our hearts, slap us across the head with our forever?

"I love you, India," Ingram whispers as he kisses my neck and slowly turns my face toward his. I smile as we kiss, and then giggle when heavily tinted screens slide up on all the back windows, giving us our own little honeymoon suite.

"I love you too, Ingram," I whisper, sighing as the adrenaline slowly drains from my system. I feel my body relaxing in Ingram's arms, and slowly I allow myself to believe that we're truly at the end of the game—and finally at the beginning of our own story.

"What a helluva story to tell our kids," Ingram whispers as he runs his finger along my neck and teases his way down my cleavage.

My nipples stiffen to big points that stick out like arrowheads through my red dress, and Ingram groans as he pinches them through the cloth. Soon he's kneading my breasts with his big hands as my body sways, my back arches, my lips tremble. I'm already wet beneath my dress, and when Ingram pulls down my straps and pushes up my bra, I almost come just from how his warm breath feels against my bare breasts.

Ingram carefully takes my left nipple into his mouth, sucking firmly as he slides his hand between my legs and massages my mound through my dress and panties. I lean back and spread for his touch, and when it comes again, I come too.

"Oh, shit, Ingram!" I gasp, my eyes going wide and then rolling up in my head as his strong fingers jam my panties into my pussy as he rubs me to climax. I'm so wet I can smell my own sex heavy in the air, and the scent heightens my orgasm in the most filthy way.

Ingram seems to have noticed the feminine scent of my heat too, because with a growl he's pushed my red dress up past my hips, ripped my panties down the side-seam, and has got his face deep in my crotch,

"You taste like heaven," he whispers as he licks me all over, sucking my clit, fucking my cunt with his tongue until I'm panting like an animal. I come all over his face when he spreads my slit with his fingers and licks me with long, broad strokes while tapping my clit, totally ringing my bell like a good husband.

He goes up on his knees, my wetness still on his lips. I just smile as I reach for my husband's painfully swollen crotch, and when I unzip him he exhales in passionate relief. I turn and lean against

the door, letting Ingram straddle me as I get his
pants and underwear down far enough to free his
beast of a cock.

He's so damned hard he's dripping thick pre-cum
all over my boobs before I even get him into my
mouth. Of course, it takes me a minute to get him
all the way into my mouth, he's so thick and long.

"You all right?" he whispers, stroking my hair as
he steadies himself and looks down lovingly at his
wife with her boobs out, her naked crotch wetting
the seat, her big brown thighs spread wide.

I nod as Ingram pulls off his jacket and shirt, and
I almost choke at the beautiful sight of his bare
body, those raw muscles all pumped and primed, a
chest like a barrel, arms like cannons, a stomach flat
like a cutting board. He's all man, and he's all mine.

Slowly Ingram moves back and forth in my
mouth, and I take deep gulps of air through my
nose as he goes faster. I manage to open my throat
all the way, and with a groan he pushes his cockhead
down. He's so peaked with arousal it's driving me
wild, and I suck hard as I reach beneath him and
gently cup his heavy balls.

That tender touch while I suck him hard takes
Ingram over the edge, and he punches into the

ceiling fabric and rips it up as he comes down my throat with a roar. With his other hand he grabs my hair and holds my head back as he finishes, and I swallow as much as I can before gasping and pulling away.

Ingram drags his throbbing cock down along my breasts, coating my dark nipples with his white semen like a beast marking his mate. Then he's back down between my legs like he's still hungry for my sex, and when I feel his hands slide under my ass and spread my buttcheeks, I slide down onto my back and let him spread my legs so wide I've got one foot up near the back windshield.

He fingers me in both holes, getting me so hot and wet I'm thrashing and mumbling, writhing and wailing, coming again and again like a switch just got flipped. Then I feel him line that cockhead up against my slit, and I gasp when I realize how hard he got for me again, how hard he's gonna take me again.

9
INGRAM

I want to take her hard, but I force myself to stay in control. She's the perfect size for a man like me, but after all the adrenaline and action of the day I need to pace myself.

But it's fucking hard to hold back from taking my wife like I want, I think as I slide into her magnificently warm pussy and flex inside her so I can feel her inner walls. She's soft and smooth, tight around my cock like we've been designed for each other. I just came like a racehorse in her mouth, but my balls still feel heavy and ready, like I'm only just getting started.

I slide my hand around the back of her head to support her, and then I brace myself and start to pump. The feeling of entering her so deep while I gaze into her eyes is almost too much to handle, and I grit my teeth as I try to hold back my orgasm so I can savor this moment.

But when India arches her head back in ecstasy and licks her red lips like she can't help it, I'm so turned on by her beauty that I explode in her like a geyser, my climax almost shattering my body, almost splintering my soul. My vision blurs as I come inside my hot-as-hell wife, and I pound into her as I give her everything I have.

She's coming too, screaming and thrashing as she claws at my bare chest like a curvy little she-beast. I slam into her one last time and hold myself there balls-deep, my muscular ass tensing up as I empty into her until she overflows down my shaft, all over the car seat that I hope isn't real leather.

We come together like unicorns mating in the clouds, and finally I collapse on my curvy bride, smothering her with my heavy body, panting against her neck, grinning like a fiend.

"Holy crap, is this what I have to look forward to every day and night for the rest of my life?" I whisper as I nibble her ear and nuzzle her neck.

"Or the rest of my life, whichever ends first," she says.

My back stiffens at the response, but I refuse to

allow myself to think about Mother and Father and the game. Since it's past sunset and we're still alive it means we're done, right? Maybe they even return our money, now that we've learned our lesson. Though I'm almost looking forward to the challenge of working my way up from scratch again. Like the saying goes: It's the journey, not the destination.

Just then both our phones beep, and I grab mine and check as my pulse races.

You've arrived at your destination, but the journey goes on forever. Congratulations. Love, Mother and Father.

I try to make sense of it, but I'm distracted by a slew of new messages from my accountants and lawyers and everyone in between.

"My billions are back," I say softly, scrolling through the messages in disbelief. One look at India and I see that she's got her stuff back too, and we collapse into each other's arms in relief.

But the relief isn't so much that we got our money back, it occurs to me after some reflection. We're relieved because it means the game is over. It means we learned what we needed to learn. We found the source of true wealth, and the money means nothing in comparison. Hell, I'm tempted to give it all away, in fact! Fuck, maybe I will! Hayes would laugh his ass off! What's up with Hayes, anyway?

Bastard hasn't returned my calls or texts. Where did he disappear to?

"Where do you want to disappear to?" India whispers against my cheek as the car makes a loop like it's waiting for instructions.

I raise an eyebrow and grin when I remember that being a billionaire does have some perks when it comes to honeymoons. "Anywhere my wife wants."

India thinks a moment, and then she whispers in my ear.

I look at her to see if she's serious. She is, and I just shake my head and shrug.

"We barely make it out of the frying pan, and my wife wants to hold my hand and lead me straight into the fucking fire," I grumble.

"Don't be dramatic," she says as I call my travel agent. "India isn't *that* hot this time of year."

10
<u>SOMEWHERE IN INDIA</u>
<u>INDIA</u>

"I take it back. India is hot as hell this time of year," I say, adjusting my oversized sunglasses and pulling my hat down so hard they'll have to cut it off me.

Ingram isn't faring much better—he's a bit burned even under his gorgeous tanned skin. We packed light and flew fast—before we had a chance to question why we were headed to the one place on Earth that we should have avoided, considering the distinct possibility that James and Janelle are somewhere here hunting for Mother and Father. They must have tried hunting for us first, of course. But now their deadline has passed—International Date Line or not—which means we're no use to them. And they're no danger to us.

Maybe that's why we're here. Both Ingram and I feel the need to face Mother and Father. Not to confront them but to thank them. To express gratitude for teaching us things we didn't have the good fortune of learning from our own parents. Of course, unless we hear from them, we don't know where to look. In the meantime, I guess we'll express our gratitude in other ways.

"I think this is it," Ingram says, stopping at a gray building that I think was originally painted white. "Come on."

We head up the stairs to the small, stuffy office with a slow ceiling fan that's only pushing hot air around the room. The woman at the desk looks up at us and frowns, like she's certain we're lost.

"You guys take checks, right?" Ingram asks with a beaming smile.

The woman nods slowly, like she still isn't sure what's up. I glance up at the sign, squinting to read the English translation in the corner. Looks right. This is the charity Ingram and I agreed on. And judging by their run-down headquarters, we chose right. We've seen so many charities with lavish offices that make it clear the money isn't going to those that need it. Just like in the business world, it's the company with the modest offices that's the most motivated to deliver value to the outside world.

And that's what Ingram and I are ready to do: Contribute to the outside world, I think as we hand over our checks and watch the woman's expression change from confusion to shock to distress to pure joy.

And it's only because we sorted out our inner world that we're able to so freely give our wealth to the outside world.

There's a lightness in our step when we get back outside, and I take my hat off and breathe deep as we walk through the narrow, crowded streets of this Indian city. We kept enough money to enjoy our vacation and then some, but we're no longer millionaires.

We're just a happily married couple who got a head start from Mother and Father.

11
ONE YEAR LATER
INGRAM

"Nothing from Mother and Father? Nah, nothing here either," I say to Hayes over the phone. I finally got in touch with him after almost a year of silence, and boy was I shocked to find out Hayes and Hannah gave their money away just like we did!

"Actually they outdid us," I complain to India after hanging up. "They gave away every last bit and committed to working their way through life. It's surreal. Hayes Henley is the head waiter at an Italian restaurant—and get this: He fucking *loves* it!" I shake my head at being outdone by my old buddy, but then I smile when I hear our quadruplets all wake up at the same time.

"At least I outdid Hayes where it counts. He only managed triplets," I say as we both head for the kids. I scoop up Ina and Ingrid while India cradles Istan and Iden against her breasts that are so full with milk I'm drooling like a sick, perverted bastard.

"Didn't know you guys had a sperm competition going," India says with a eye-roll. But her eyelids flick wide open and stay open when she sees the rise in my crotch as she bares her breasts to feed our hungry little critters.

Ina and Ingrid doze off in my arms, and I gently put them back in their rockers before heading to my post-pregnant wife who's glowing like an oasis in the desert of my world. I kiss her neck from behind as she feeds our babies, and soon I slyly reach under her loose dress and gently massage her mound through her panties.

She's wet for me in a moment, and I silently grind my cock against her soft ass until she's pushing back against me and getting me harder than the stone wall of the country farmhouse we decided to make our home. We wanted to raise our kids away from the city, and this worked out perfectly. I never thought we could work the land, but it came so naturally I wonder if it was in our blood.

But soon the blood leaves my brain to fill my cock, and all my thoughts dissolve in an ocean of pure bliss when India tucks the kids away, raises her arms, and lets me suck on her milky breasts like the dirty Daddy I am.

I drink her sweet cream until she gasps and goes limp in my arms, and I smile and carry her outside to the open porch that faces the backyard forest. I only bring her out here when I know it's gonna get too loud for the kids, and when she feels me rip off her milk-stained dress and yank her panties off her wide hips, she leans against a pillar and pushes me down to my knees.

"Down, boy," she mutters as I grin and lick her between the legs.

"Careful, little girl," I growl as slide my tongue into her and reach around for that divine ass that's even more luscious from the weight she gained from carrying four of my babies around for nine months. "I'm a wild animal, not a fucking house pet."

"I'm the mother of your children," she gasps, curling her tongue over her upper lip as I bring forth her wetness until the tang of her cunt overwhelms the sweetness of her cream in my mouth. "You'll do what I say."

I slap her thighs in response, and she yelps and

swats me on the head. I grin and do it again, smacking the sides of her bottom and then grabbing her ass and spreading those cheeks as I look up at her.

"Well, I'm the father of your children, and you'll obey when I command," I growl.

"You're not very scary when you're down on your knees, milk all over your beard like a filthy—"

But India can't finish, because in one swift movement I bring her down to *her* knees, and before she can say "Filthy Father" I've got Mother spread across my lap, ass in the air, and I'm spanking her good and hard with rough farmer's hands.

She screams into the depths of the forest as I tame the she-wolf in her, and then I'm inside her from behind, her ass taming the alpha wolf in me.

I come hard like I always do, emptying my balls deep in her ass, filling her until she overflows. I rub her from beneath, but she's already coming, and I just smile and finger her until she goes over the edge like a freight train running out of track.

I stroke her hair and kiss her neck, flattening her with my weight as I collapse on her from behind. Then I caress her sides, massage her body, and kiss her lips as we enjoy the peace of the woods.

And then it happens.

Both our phones beep at once.

And we just smile as the thrill of the past awakens in us again.

We've been waiting for the call.

Waiting for the message.

Waiting for an invitation . . .

To the family reunion.

∞

EPILOGUE
<u>MOTHER AND FATHER</u>

"**D**id you send out the invitations?" says Mother.

"What do you think?" says Father.

"Are all the kids coming?" says Mother.

"What do you think?" says Father.

"Do you think they'll be surprised to see what happened with James and Janelle?" says Mother.

"What do you think?" says Father.

And they both laugh.

∞

FROM THE AUTHOR

James and Janelle's story ends this trilogy
in BILLIONAIRE'S CURVY CONTRACT!

And in case you missed it, my DRAGON'S
CURVY MATE Series is complete!

Love,
Anna.

∞

Books by Annabelle Winters

The CURVES FOR SHEIKHS Series

Curves for the Sheikh
Flames for the Sheikh
Hostage for the Sheikh
Single for the Sheikh
Stockings for the Sheikh
Untouched for the Sheikh
Surrogate for the Sheikh
Stars for the Sheikh
Shelter for the Sheikh
Shared for the Sheikh
Assassin for the Sheikh
Privilege for the Sheikh
Ransomed for the Sheikh
Uncorked for the Sheikh
Haunted for the Sheikh
Grateful for the Sheikh
Mistletoe for the Sheikh
Fake for the Sheikh

The CURVES FOR SHIFTERS Series

Curves for the Dragon
Born for the Bear
Witch for the Wolf
Tamed for the Lion
Taken for the Tiger

The CURVY FOR HIM Series

The Teacher and the Trainer
The Librarian and the Cop
The Lawyer and the Cowboy
The Princess and the Pirate

The CEO and the Soldier
The Astronaut and the Alien
The Botanist and the Biker
The Psychic and the Senator

The CURVY FOR THE HOLIDAYS Series
Taken on Thanksgiving
Captive for Christmas
Night Before New Year's
Vampire's Curvy Valentine
Flagged on the Fourth
Home for Halloween

The CURVY FOR KEEPS Series
Summoned by the CEO
Given to the Groom

The DRAGON'S CURVY MATE Series
Dragon's Curvy Assistant
Dragon's Curvy Banker
Dragon's Curvy Counselor
Dragon's Curvy Doctor
Dragon's Curvy Engineer
Dragon's Curvy Firefighter
Dragon's Curvy Gambler

The CURVY IN COLLEGE Series
The Jock and the Genius
The Rockstar and the Recluse
The Dropout and the Debutante
The Player and the Princess
The Fratboy and the Feminist

WWW.ANNABELLEWINTERS.

Printed in Dunstable, United Kingdom

63954876R00058